Little (

A series of heart warming short stories about a mixed race little girl called Gemma.

This bright and humorous little pre-schooler, shares her every day experiences with other young children and infants, in the hope that the adult sharing this story with them, will discuss any issues, fears or concerns raised. This will support the development of the child's social and emotional intelligence. Having an opportunity to discuss fears and anxieties can reduce stress and encourage positive mental health and a sense of well being.

To all of the staff and
pre-schoolers at Hollywood
Pre-School.

Thanks for all of your
support and for believing in
me.

Thank you also, for giving
my three children the best
start in education.

This book was written for my children before my first child was born.

All of my children love these funny stories and we talk for ages about the issues raised.

I am sure that children everywhere will love these stories too.

Look carefully at each picture.
They are all the same you might say – but look again!

Spot all the differences and send the answers to
browncherub@hotmail.com
with your name, age and address to win a free prize.

Reading is fun!
The illustrations are in black and white so that your child can explore their own creative talents and colour them in as they wish. Can they make each picture different? Then you could add a picture of your own to show a happy ending.

Enjoy!

<u>He Took My Book</u>

Yesterday at pre - school,
I chose my favourite book.
Jaypal sat beside me.
And asked if he could look.

I said "Yes," to Jaypal.
I let him have a look.
But Jaypal got up
and walked away,
And he took my book.

"No, Jaypal," I cried out.
"You can't take it away.
I haven't finished with it yet.
Listen to what I say."

But Jaypal walked away with it.
As if I was not there.
And I felt all alone, by myself,
sitting in the chair.

I didn't know what to do,
I was trying not to cry.
I had to get my book back.
I knew I had to try.

I walked across the classroom,
Jaypal was sitting there.
He looked up and
smiled at me.
I gave a nasty stare.

"Give me back my book,
Jaypal,
Give it to me now!"
I knew I had to get it back.
But I wasn't quite sure how.

"No, Gem," he said,
"I'm keeping it,
I won't give it back to you.
I don't have to listen!
There's nothing you can do!"

I grabbed the book
from Jaypal.
I pulled with all my might.
He tried to stand,
I pushed him down.
And we began to fight.

He slapped me on my arm.
So I pulled his hair.
We rolled about and
tore the book.
But we didn't care.

Our teacher stopped
us fighting.
We said sorry to each other.
Then we had to
mend the book.
And go and choose another.

Author
Myrah Duckworth
B.Ed Hons

Teacher (1996)
Life coach & mentor

I have been writing books for children and young people for over twelve years. Finally, I feel it's time to share them with the world!

Having worked with children for more than twenty years and raising three children of my own, I know that both the young and old have many concerns and issues that they don't always get an opportunity to discuss. These lovely stories provide that opportunity.

I live in Birmingham with my three beautiful children and my amazing fiancé.

My family and friends are my world.

Thanks to you all. Thanks to Teswal and Cheryl for believing in this project. Thanks Tony L. Brown for lighting the way. Thanks to The Most High for blessing me with this creative talent.

<u>Illustrator</u>
Mayuko Taniguchi

Self taught artist & illustrator
Mayuko lives in Japan with her gorgeous son and loving husband.

Proof-reader
Annika Rowbury-Harrison

Teacher of languages

Recommendations
Chris & Rachel Hemming
Just The Two Of Us Child-Minding

I think they all have valuable messages, and I loved them all.

Steven Brown B.Phil. Community, Youth and Play Work

With over 20 years of formal and informal education with toddlers, children, young people, adults, parents and families, Little Gem's are so refreshing and inclusive. Written with grace, sensitivity and understanding of the target audience and need for explanation of taboo subjects, such as step families, mixed ethnicity and other things children often question. I can already see the animated version; these stories really are little Gems.

Toni-Anne Butterworth-Myers B.SC, M.SC, Family Worker, Trainee Occupational Psychologist

I have worked with various parents around parenting for connecting emotionally and socially with their children and part of this has included emphasising the importance of reading to their children as a form of bonding. The Little Gems books in particular really offer the parents the opportunity to step into the world of children since
Gem speaks so openly, honestly and innocently about real-life childhood experiences which can be considered to be of a sensitive nature. They address much needed family issues which need to be

spoken about in schools and families and also represent the current family settings. I thoroughly enjoyed the collection and am pleased to share them all with my own child.

Other titles in the Little Gem's series include:
Mummy's Lost
Where Is Teddy?
I'm Not Scared
Dinner Wars
... and many others.

Sponsored by my favourite lovely lady in the whole world. Thank you so much for believing in me. Without you, none of this would have been possible.

Printed in Great Britain
by Amazon